D1120214

The Nine Lives of Dudley Dog

John and Ann Hassett

 Houghton Mifflin Company Boston 2008   Walter Lorraine Books

For Jimbo

Walter Lorraine (wl) Books

www.houghtonmifflinbooks.com

Library of Congress Cataloging-in-Publication Data

Hassett, John.
  The nine lives of Dudley Dog / by John and Ann Hassett.
      p. cm.
  "Walter Lorraine books."
  Summary: A persistent dog chases one cat after another, paying no heed to the dangers
  of busy streets, trains, bees, bulldozers, skunks, or raging fires.
  ISBN-13: 978-0-618-81153-3
  ISBN-10: 0-618-81153-2
  [1. Dogs—Fiction. 2. Cats—Fiction. 3. Safety—Fiction.] I. Hassett, Ann (Ann M.) II. Title.
  PZ7.H2785Ni 2008
  [E]—dc22

                                                              2007019598

Printed in Singapore
TWP   10 9 8 7 6 5 4 3 2 1

The Nine Lives of

Dudley Dog

Dudley was a dog.
Sister had wanted a cat
for her birthday,
but there had
been a mix-up
at the pet store.

Sister frowned
and blew out
the candles
on her cake.
"Did you make
a wish?" asked
Mother and Father.
"I certainly did,"
she said.

Dudley jumped
out the window.
He began
to chase cats.

Dudley chased a cat
across a busy street.
He did not look
both ways.
Cars beeped.
Angry drivers
shouted and shook
their fists.
"Bad dog,"
scolded a taxidriver.
"Do you think
you have nine lives
like a cat?"

11

12

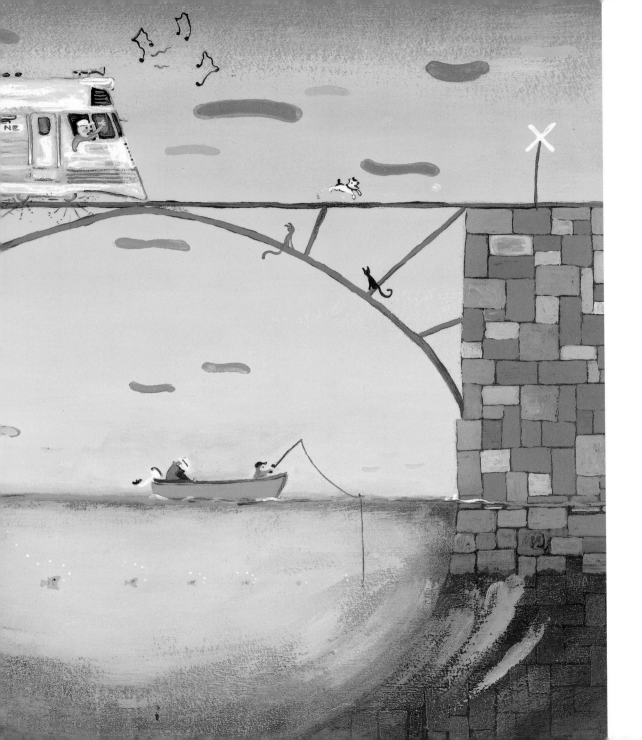

Dudley chased cats
on the railroad tracks.
A hurrying train
blasted its horn,
then *screeeeeeeched*
to a stop.
"Bad dog,"
scolded the engineer.
"Do you think
you have nine lives
like a cat?"

Dudley chased cats
in the park.
He trampled
the flowers.
He bothered
the bees.
Angry bees
buzzed
after Dudley.
"Bad dog,"
scolded a babysitter.
"Do you think
you have nine lives
like a cat?"

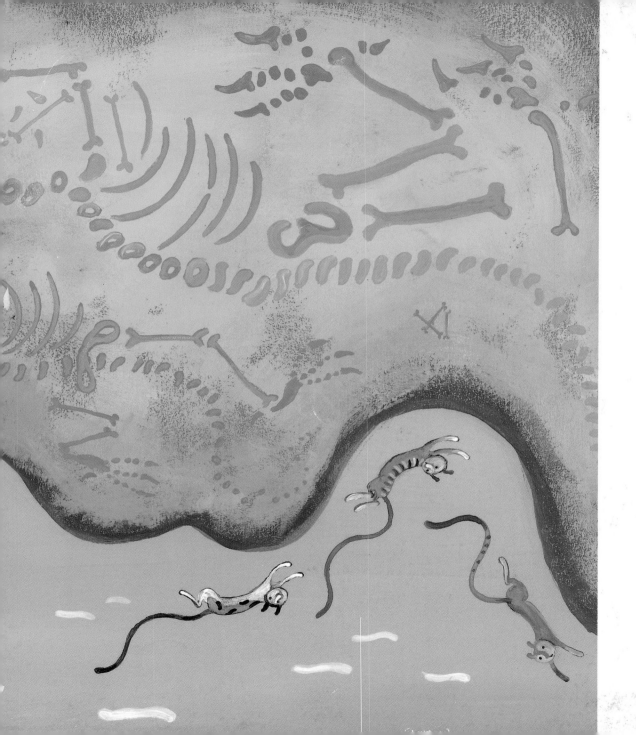

Dudley chased cats
past bulldozers
and big trucks.
The ground shook
like an earthquake.
Dudley dropped
into a hole.
"Bad dog,"
scolded a worker.
"Do you think
you have nine lives
like a cat?"

Dudley chased
skunks he mistook
for cats.
The chase
was short.
"Bad dog,"
scolded a paperboy,
holding his nose.
"Do you think
you have nine lives
like a cat?"

Dudley chased cats
into a burning building.
Sparks scorched
his fur. Firefighters
plucked Dudley
from the smoke.
"Bad dog,"
scolded a fireman.
"Do you think
you have nine lives
like a cat?"

Dudley chased cats
past a swimming pool.
Dudley fell in —
he could not swim.
He sank like a stone.
"Bad dog,"
scolded a grandmother.
"Do you think
you have nine lives
like a cat?"

Dudley chased cats
in a thunderstorm.
Lightning flashed.
The sky rumbled.
The wind blew
like a hurricane.
"Bad dog,"
scolded a mailman.
"Do you think
you have nine lives
like a cat?"

Dudley chased cats
at the circus.
Too bad for Dudley —
circus cats
have stripes,
and they
are called tigers.

That night,
a cat hopped
in the window.
The cat
looked
strangely
familiar.
Strangest
of all,
the cat
was wearing
Dudley's collar.

Sister's
birthday
wish
had
come
true.